Christopher Is Not Afraid...Anymore

Craig Burris

Illustrated by Priscilla Burris

THOMAS NELSON PUBLISHERS
Nashville • Atlanta • London • Vancouver

Christopher Crumpkin
was just a little guy.

Whenever something
scared him he would
cry, cry, cry.

Christopher Is Not Afraid ...Anymore

Published in Nashville, Tennessee, by Thomas Nelson, Inc., Publishers, and dis-
tributed in Canada by Word Communications, Ltd., Richmond, British
Columbia.

The Bible verse used in this publication is from THE NEW KING JAMES
VERSION. Copyright © 1979, 1980, 1982, Thomas Nelson, Inc., Publishers.

ISBN 0-7852-7978-4

Printed in the United States of America.

1 2 3 4 5 6 7 —00 99 98 97 96 95 94

Dogs that would growl and bark.

Being alone in his room after dark.

Bugs that would jump or creep.

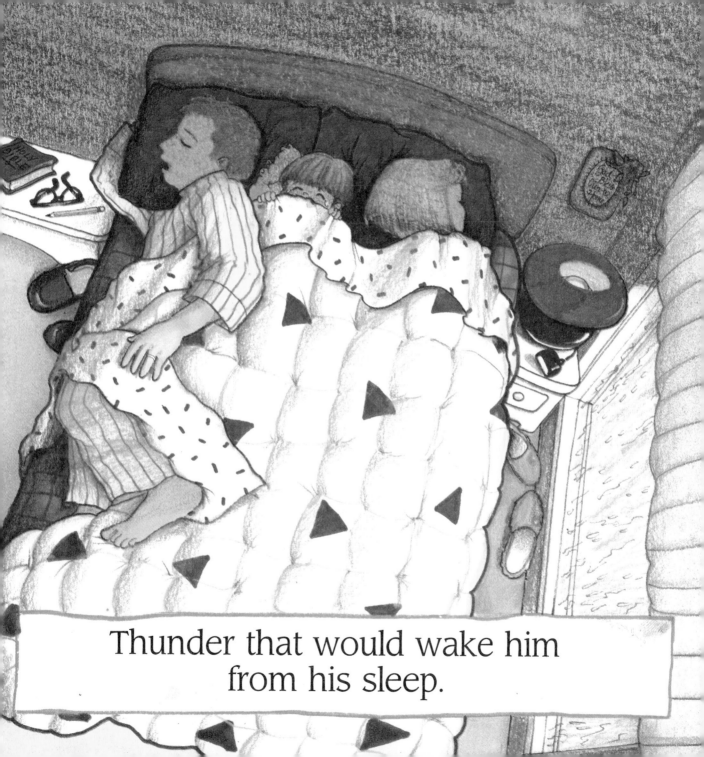

Thunder that would wake him
from his sleep.

Stories he heard that made him feel worried inside.

Shadows he saw
that made his eyes open wide.

The kids he played with would tease him and call him names.

Christopher would cry and run home. He was so ashamed.

Then one day his mom said, "Go to the kitchen and wait for me there."

Christopher slowly walked in and sat down on his chair.

At first he thought she wanted him to help her cook.
Instead she went to her room and came back with a book.

She looked for her glasses and found
them in her purse.
Then she opened the book, found the
right chapter, then the right verse.
She said, "Whenever you don't feel
safe and secure,
remember one thing—of this
you can be sure.

"God has written in the Bible something marvelous. "It says that He is stronger than anything that can harm us.

"Take some time to remember this verse.
"It will make you feel better
when things seem worse."

"The LORD is my light and my salvation; whom shall I fear?

The LORD is the strength of my life; of whom shall I be afraid?"

Psalm 27:1

Christopher's eyes brightened as his mom read it one more time.
Then she wrote it on some paper and said, "Repeat it in your mind."

Christopher took the paper and read the words from beginning to end. Then he closed his eyes and said the verse again and again.

I know that God loves me and what's written in the Bible is true.
Now I know a promise. When I'm scared I'll know what to do.

Christopher repeated the verse
over and over.
He even said it out loud to his
pet named Rover.

One day he climbed a tree with his best friend, Jake.

When it was time to come down
their knees began to shake.

"The Lord is the strength of my life,"
Christopher said prayerfully.
He took a deep breath and climbed
down very carefully.

Christopher was standing on the
ground before he knew it.
Then he looked up at Jake and said,
"Come on, you can do it."

"It's too high, I might fall,"
    Jake said with despair.
"That's all right," Christopher said,
    "I know a verse that I'll share."

When Jake got down he thanked Christopher for his help.
Then they raced home to have some cookies and milk.